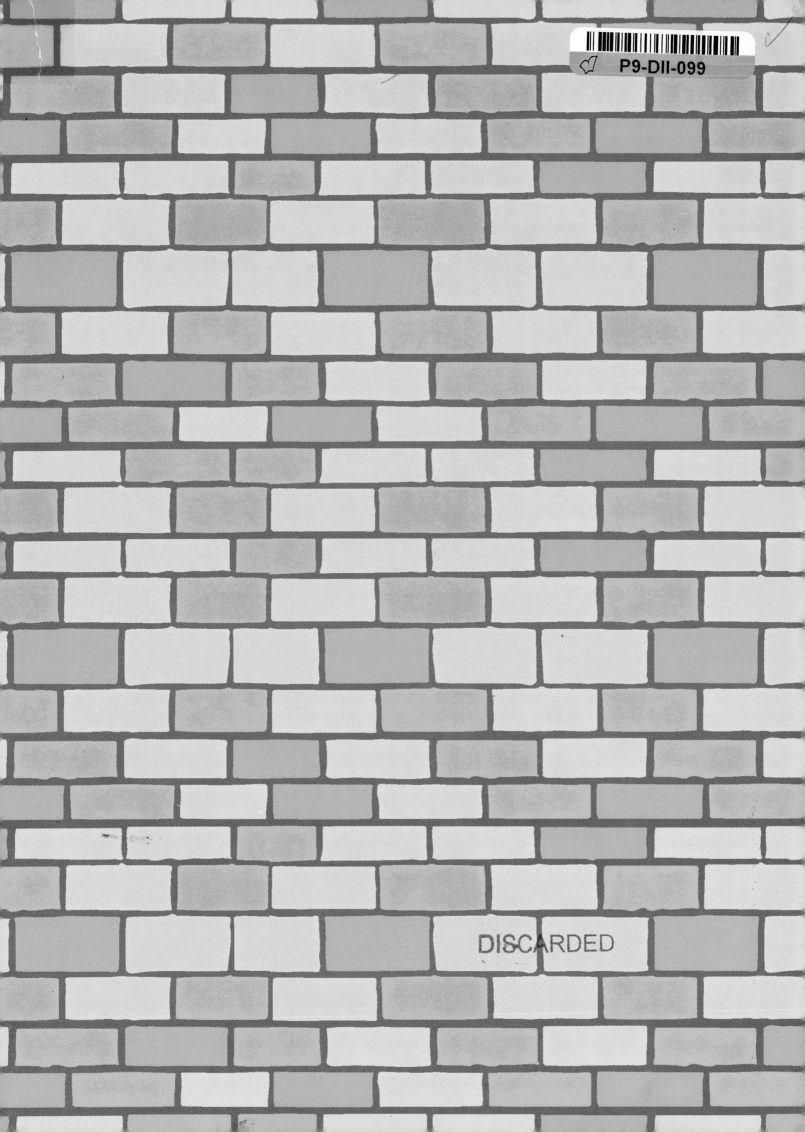

Bob the Builder ™

This book belongs to:

Bob's Big
Story
Collection

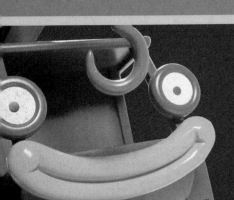

I hope you enjoy this book. There are two types of stories in the collection—the **short** stories are just right to dip into, and there are **longer** ones which make perfect bedtime stories!

Can you read it?
Yes, you can!

Pilchard Goes Fishing

Muck and Scoop could hear some very strange noises coming from inside Bob's house.

"Keep still! Honestly!" they heard Bob say.

"I wonder what's going on," said Scoop.

"Morning, everyone!" called Wendy when she arrived at the yard. "Where's Bob?"

"He's in the house, but we don't know what he's doing," replied Muck.

"It's no use wriggling like that . . . ," they could hear Bob saying.

Wendy went in to find out what was going on.

"Bob! What are you doing?" asked Wendy.

"I thought it was time that I cleaned out Finn's tank. Only, he's not helping, are you, Finn?" said Bob.

"It doesn't look easy," said Wendy as she watched Bob trying to catch the goldfish in a little net.

Pilchard watched Bob and Finn and licked her lips.

6

"Oh, no, look at the time!" said Bob as he put the net down and grabbed his hat.

"Don't worry, you get going. I'll deal with Finn. I'll see you later," Wendy said as Bob dashed out.

"**Meow!**" Pilchard said. She was still watching the tank very carefully.

"Yes, I know, Pilchard," said Wendy. "I'll just sort out a few things in the office, then we'll clean Finn's tank!"

"**Meow!**" said Pilchard very loudly.

Bob rushed out of the house and started to organize the machines.

"Come on, everyone! We've got lots of different jobs to do today. Muck, I'll need you to help me, and I'll need Dizzy and Roley too," he said.

"**Can we fix it?**" called Scoop.

"**Yes, we can!**" everyone shouted. Bob jumped onto Muck's step, and they took off.

Bob and the team pulled up in front of
the tunnel.

"Shall I start mixing, Bob?" asked Dizzy.

"Yes, Dizzy. You do that. . . . Oh, no! I've
forgotten the cement. Muck, would you
mind going back to the yard and
getting a couple of bags of cement,
please?" asked Bob.

"On my way, Bob!" said Muck happily,
driving off.

"Please hurry! We've got lots to do today!"
Bob called after Muck.

"Now, come on, Finn," said Wendy. "That's it!" she said as she scooped him into the net. "I'll just put you somewhere safe," she added, flopping Finn into a bucket of water.

"**Meow!**" said Pilchard as she watched Wendy.

Just then there was a loud screeching noise out in the yard.

"Oh, that sounds like Muck," said Wendy. She grabbed the bucket and rushed outside.

She was just in time to see Muck swerve to avoid Bird, then skid across the yard and bang into the lean-to. The wooden support broke and fell into Muck's front scoop.

Wendy rushed over. "Are you all right, Muck?"

"I'm okay. I'm sorry. Bob sent me back for some cement and he said to hurry, so I did and went a bit fast and . . . you won't tell Bob, will you?" said Muck.

"Oh, Muck. Bob would understand," said Wendy.

"*Pleeease*, Wendy, I feel silly," said Muck.

"Okay, I won't tell him," agreed Wendy.

"The lean-to shouldn't be too hard to fix," said Wendy. "Here's the cement," she added as she put the sacks in Muck's front scoop.

"Thanks, Wendy!" Muck called, rushing back to the job site.

Wendy loosened what was left of the wooden support and tied some rope tightly around it.

"Now, Lofty, it's your turn. Can you help me pull the broken stump out of the ground?" asked Wendy.

"Oh, um . . . yes. . . . I think so," muttered Lofty as he swung his hook into place.

"Okay, pull!" called Wendy. And Lofty began to heave.

While Wendy was busy, Pilchard placed her front paws on the bucket and watched Finn. She was just about to dip a paw into the water when the stump came free.

"Well done, Lofty!" cried Wendy.

But Lofty had trouble controlling his arm, and the stump flew toward Pilchard.

"**Yeeoow!**" yelped Pilchard as she ran away.

Wendy found Bob's drill and climbed the ladder to fasten the new wooden post to the roof.

Pilchard saw that Wendy was busy and crept up to the bucket again. She peered down at Finn.

When Bob arrived back at the yard a short while later, Wendy was still on the ladder. Pilchard ran and hid behind Scoop.

"There, all done!" Wendy said, climbing down.

"Hello, Wendy," called Bob. "What are you up to?"

"Ummm," she said.

"I had a little accident, Bob," said Muck, owning up.

"It wasn't Muck's fault," added Scoop.

"I skidded to miss Bird, and I bashed right into the lean-to," explained Muck. "Sorry, Bob."

"There's no need to be sorry. You didn't do it on purpose, and Bird's fine," said Bob.

"It's as good as new!" Bob continued as he and Muck inspected the lean-to. "Wendy, our brilliant builder, has fixed it!"

"I couldn't have done it without Lofty's help!" Wendy said.

While everyone was admiring the lean-to, Pilchard crept back to the bucket. This time she was determined to catch Finn. She dipped her paw into the water . . . but Bird was on top of the lean-to and spotted Pilchard.

He gave a loud "**Toot, toot!**" to catch everyone's attention.

"**Meeeeeoow!**" yelped Pilchard as she jumped back and ran away.

Wendy rushed over. "Oh, Pilchard! Bird! I'd completely forgotten about poor Finn! What a clever cat—and what a clever bird!

"There's been so much excitement with the lean-to, I'd forgotten I was cleaning out the fish tank. But Pilchard and Bird just reminded me."

"**Meow!**" said Pilchard crossly.

"There you go, Finn. Your tank is all nice and clean again," said Bob as he scooped up Finn from the bucket and dropped him into the tank. Pilchard prowled around the living room.

"Pilchard!" called Wendy. "I've got a little reward for you, for being such a clever cat. Look, a lovely fish for your dinner!"

Pilchard had had quite enough of fish for one day and sank to the floor.

"**Meow, wowww, wowww!**" she moaned.

"I wonder what's up with Pilchard," said Bob, puzzled.

"At least Finn's pleased," said Wendy as Finn did a perfect back flip in his lovely, clean tank.

THE END!

Lofty to the Rescue

Bob and the team were fixing the potholes in a country road, but they had to stop when they came to a bridge that was blocked by logs and bricks.

"Oh, dear! We'll have to clear this before we can get to work on the road," said Bob.

"**Can we clear it?**" asked Scoop.

"**Yes, we can!**" cried Bob, Dizzy, and Lofty.

Everyone got right to work clearing the bridge, except for Lofty.

"Um, I'm scared of heights," he said, looking at the bridge nervously. "I think I'll find another way around," Lofty said as he started to back away.

Spud jumped out from behind a bush. "Hee, hee! Lofty's scared of heights!" he teased.

"Hey, Spud," called Scoop. "Stop it! Leave him alone."

But Spud ignored him and started to make mud pies to throw at Lofty.

"Nyah, nyah, nyah! Lofty's a scaredy-crane!" Spud called as Lofty took off.

Spud jumped up and down calling after Lofty, but then he slipped . . . wobbled . . . and fell—right over the side of the bridge! "**Whhhhhhhooooaaaaa!**" he shouted.

Luckily Spud didn't fall too far. His pants got caught on a branch. The machines gathered around him.

"Help!" Spud screamed.

"How are we going to rescue him?" asked Muck.

"The only one who can reach that far is Lofty," said Scoop.

"Hang in there, Spud! I'll try to catch up with Lofty," shouted Muck, speeding away.

Muck finally found Lofty.
"Please come and help," begged Muck.

"Spud was very unkind. But if he's in trouble, I suppose I should," said Lofty, looking very worried.

They went back to the bridge.

Suddenly the branch made a loud **crack!**

"You'll have to be quick, Lofty," said Bob. "Lower your crane. Easy does it!"

"Ohhh, I can't look," whimpered Lofty. "Bob, you'll have to tell me what to do."

"**Oh, ohhhh!**" wailed Spud as the branch began to give way under his weight.

"Forward a bit, Lofty," Bob called. "Now lower your hook."

Lofty edged his hook closer to Spud and slipped it through Spud's belt.

The rest of the team watched from below the bridge until Spud was lifted safely back onto it.

"**Hooray!**" they all cheered when the rescue was over.

"Nice one, Lofty," said Scoop.

"Oh? Did I do it?" asked Lofty.

"Of course you did, Lofty. You can open your eyes now," said Bob.

Lofty opened his eyes to find everyone grinning at him.

"I think Spud has something to say to you, don't you Spud?" said Bob.

"Um, yeah. Thanks, Lofty, and sorry about teasing you," said Spud.

"You saved the day, Lofty!" said Bob.
Lofty smiled. He wasn't a scaredy-crane after all!

THE END!

Bob's Bugle

Bob the Builder was busy fixing a broken central heating system. Muck was helping him.
"I've finished the boiler," said Bob, going downstairs. "Now for the new hot-water tank."
Muck helped Bob get the tank out of the back tipper and the pipes from the front scoop. Bob quickly attached them to the boiler.
"Now it's time to check the pipes," Bob said.

One of the pipes was blocked by a little bit of dirt. Bob blew into the pipe, and the dirt popped out.

Blurgh-boo-boo-blooooh! whistled the pipe as Bob blew through it.

"I like that," said Bob with a laugh.

"Bob? Are you all right in there?" called Muck anxiously.

"Yes, I'm fine," Bob replied. "Listen to this, Muck."

T-o-o-o-o-t-tee-toooot-tooot!

"What is it . . . a frog with a sore throat?" Muck asked.

"No!" said Bob excitedly. "It's my bugle! Or, it will be, when I'm finished making it."

"What's a bugle?" Muck asked.

"It's a musical instrument," Bob explained. "You blow into one end, and a loud noise comes out of the other. Listen!" Bob gave another blast into the pipe. **Parrrrrp-tee-ti-tee-toooot-tooooot!**

Back at the yard, Wendy was looking very thoughtful.

"Some friends of mine have just moved into a new house, and I'd really like to give them something special. But I can't think of anything!" Wendy told Lofty.

Pilchard pushed her wind-up mouse toward Wendy.

"That's very kind," Wendy said. "But I don't think my friends really need a wind-up mouse."

Just then Muck and Bob roared into the yard.

"Guess what?" Muck yelled. "Bob's going to make a bugle!"

Bob hurried into his workshop and shut the door. The machines clustered around outside. They heard bangs and clanks. Then suddenly a loud **parp!** made them all jump.

"How about this, then?" Bob asked, and he came out waving his new bugle. He put it to his mouth and blew:

Bloohoooowoopaarp!

"What's that awful noise?" cried Wendy, rushing out of her office with her hands clamped over her ears.

"Shhh, Wendy," whispered Scoop. "It's Bob's new bugle, and he thinks it's great."

"It's terrible!" cried Wendy.

"It's great!" rumbled Roley.

"Really?" Bob chuckled. "Perhaps I could join a band!"

"You'll have to practice hard," said Roley.

"You're right," agreed Bob.

"Can I practice? Yes, I can!"

Bob practiced his bugle all night long.
Blooo-hooo-dooo-diddley-diddley-dooo!
"I want to go to sleep!" wailed Muck.
"Perhaps we should say something to Bob,"
Lofty mumbled.
"Bob's just having fun!" rumbled Roley.
The tired machines listened as the
loud bugle blasts slowly turned to
weak **toot-toots**, then one last
paaaarp.
"He's stopped!" gasped Dizzy.
"Thank goodness for that," Muck
said with a yawn.

The next morning Wendy told the machines, "I hardly slept last night, worrying about what present to get my friends."

"We hardly slept last night because of Bob playing his bugle!" grumbled Muck.

"He'll be tired this morning," said Wendy.

But Bob wasn't the least bit tired. He strolled across the yard, playing his bugle. The noise sounded like an elephant blowing its nose.

"Come on, Muck! We've got work to do," Bob said as he put his bugle by the door of the workshop.

"Now's our chance, Lofty!" said Scoop. "Grab the bugle!"

"Whoa," Lofty said as he extended his crane and hooked the bugle on to the end.

"Bob will never find it on the roof," Dizzy said.

Lofty carefully put it on the roof. But then Bird hopped over to the bugle and started to peck at it. The bugle rolled forward.

"Look out!" cried Muck. The bugle rolled off the roof and landed in Muck's scoop.

"What was that?" called Bob, coming out of the workshop.

"Nothing!" said Muck.

"Come on, Muck," said Bob. "We've got to finish that central heating job."

While Bob packed up his tools, Muck hunted around for somewhere to hide the bugle.

Dizzy ran up and tipped her mixer forward. "I'll take it," she whispered.

"Phew . . . what a relief," Muck said with a sigh. But then disaster struck!

"Dizzy," called Bob. "I'll need you, too!"

Dizzy's face fell. "Me?!" she exclaimed. "Oh, no!"

At the house, Bob went inside to fix the radiators, singing as he worked.

Outside, Dizzy and Muck wondered what to do.

"Can't you just leave the bugle somewhere?" asked Muck.

"I can't do that!" protested Dizzy.

Suddenly Bob appeared at the door with a bucket.

"Cement please, Dizzy," he said.

"Are you sure?" Dizzy asked.

"Of course I'm sure!" Bob replied, laughing.

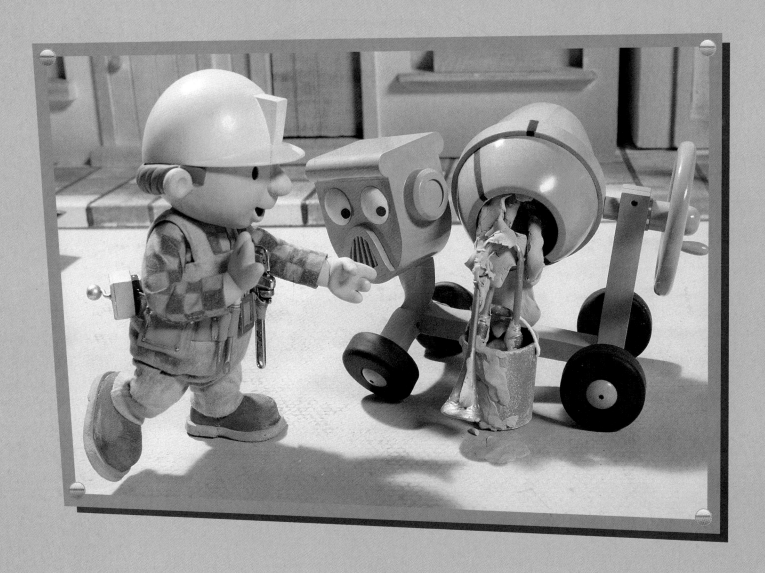

"Here goes . . . ," said Dizzy. She poured a load of cement into Bob's bucket. **Glug-glug-CLANG!**

Bob couldn't believe his eyes when he saw his bugle covered in cement.

"How did that get in there?" he cried.

Muck and Dizzy pretended to be surprised.

"I've no idea!" squeaked Dizzy.

"Me neither," said Muck firmly.

"Oh, well," said Bob. "No harm done. I'll soon have it cleaned up."

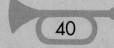

Back at the yard, Bob wiped the sticky cement off his bugle. Then he put it on the ground.

"Can you come over here, Roley?" Bob asked.

"Okay, Bob," rumbled Roley, as he moved forward. But Roley didn't look where he was going.

Crunch! Roley rolled right over Bob's bugle!

"What was that noise?" asked Bob.

Roley stared down at the flattened bugle.

"It's your bugle, Bob," he groaned. "I'm so sorry. . . . I flattened it!"

Although Bob felt sad, he could see that Roley was really very upset.

"Don't worry, Roley," he said. "I shouldn't have left it lying around like that."

Bob bent down to pick up the flattened bugle.

Tinkle . . . tinkle . . . tinkle . . . went the broken pieces.

"That's a lovely set of wind chimes," said Wendy, coming out of her office. "Just the sort of housewarming present I have been looking for."

Bob smiled at the wind chimes dangling in his hand.

"You know, there I was, thinking I'd made a bugle, when it was really a set of wind chimes! Here you are, Wendy. You can have these for your friends."

"Thank you, Bob!" cried Wendy. She gently shook the chimes. **Tinkle . . . tinkle . . . tinkle . . .**

"Ah . . . ," sighed Muck. "Nice, quiet wind chimes."

"I quite liked the bugle myself!" rumbled Roley.

THE END!

Wallpaper Wendy

"We're off to re-lay the road in front of the town hall. Is everyone ready?" asked Bob.

"**Can I roll it?**" asked Roley.

"**Yes, you can!**" shouted Muck.

Dizzy didn't hear because she was listening to music on her headphones.

"Come on, Dizzy," said Wendy. "Bob will need your help too!"

When they got to the town hall, Bob and Muck shoveled the gravel into place.

"Okay, Roley," said Muck. "We're ready for you to do your part."

"**Rock and roll!**" shouted Roley as he moved forward and crunched the gravel flat.

Mrs. Broadbent stood watching the team.
When they stopped for a break,
she rushed over to speak to Bob.

"Bob, can you help?" she asked.
"My mother is arriving tomorrow, and
the house isn't ready. My decorators
have let me down."

"Bob, you're a builder, not
a decorator," warned Muck.

"Decorating's easy!" said Bob.
"Can we fix it?"

"Um . . . yes, we can!" all the machines
answered. But they weren't sure!

Bob and Dizzy went over to Mrs. Broadbent's house right away. They didn't have much time, so they had to work quickly.

Bob tried to put paste on the wallpaper, but it wouldn't lie flat! It stuck to his hands and to the ladder but not to the wall.

Then as Bob climbed down the ladder, he put his foot right into the bucket of paste!

Dizzy tried to get Bob's foot out of the bucket, but she couldn't stop laughing. She slipped on some paste, and the bucket flew into the air and landed on Bob's head!

"This isn't as easy as I thought it would be," complained Bob.

Wendy arrived just in time. "Bob! Dizzy! What are you doing?!" she exclaimed. "Look at this mess!"

"You better go and get some lunch, and I'll see what I can do here," said Wendy.

She cleaned and washed. Then she pasted and papered. Soon the room looked lovely. Just as she finished painting the radiator, she heard a noise at the front door.

It was Mrs. Broadbent coming to see how the team was doing. Bob arrived back from lunch at the same time.

"Hello, Mrs. Broadbent. I was just telling the machines how well it was all going," said Bob guiltily. "But you can't go in. It's not . . . um . . . quite ready yet," he mumbled, remembering the mess.

But Mrs. Broadbent went in anyway. . . .

Bob was surprised to see the wallpaper up and the room neat and tidy! "Wow!" he said.

Mrs. Broadbent was thrilled!

"You've done a fabulous job, Bob. You're so clever!" she said.

"Oh, don't thank me," said Bob. "Wendy did it all. She's brilliant!"

THE END!

Roley's Tortoise

The team was building a new bus stop in the country.

"Right, Muck! We're ready for the gravel," said Wendy.

"Okay! Where do you want it?" asked Muck eagerly.

"Over here, please," she replied, pointing at a spot just in front of Roley.

Muck lowered the scoop and dumped the gravel. Wendy waved Roley forward to flatten it. "Come on, Bird! Let's rock and roll!" rumbled Roley. "**Toot!**" chirped Bird happily.

Dizzy was practicing her aerobics routine. "To the left . . . two, three, four, and **stre-e-etch**," she chanted. As she reached up she noticed something moving just in front of Roley.

"Stop, Roley! Stop!" Dizzy shouted.

Roley screeched to a halt.

"What is it, Dizzy?" asked Bob.

"Look!" said Dizzy. "There's a stone with a head, and it's moving!"

"Wow! It's a tortoise," Wendy said. "How did it get here?"

"It's a good thing you spotted him, Dizzy. We could have had a very nasty accident," said Wendy.

"Yeah," said Dizzy, smiling proudly.

The tortoise started to climb up the pile of gravel very slowly. Bird jumped down.

Roley peered at the tortoise. "You're like me, aren't you?" he said. "Slow, but you get there in the end. What are we going to do with him, Wendy?"

"I don't know, Roley, but he can't stay here while we're working. He might get hurt," Wendy replied.

"Can I take Timmy back to the yard, please?" Roley begged.

"Who's Timmy?" asked Bob.

"Timmy the tortoise. . . . That's his name!" said Roley.

"Ha, ha!" laughed Bob. "Yes, we'll keep him until we find his owner," said Bob. He picked up Timmy to keep him safe while Roley finished the job.

When they were done, Bob, Roley, and Dizzy took Timmy back to the yard.

Muck went on ahead with Lofty to collect the material for the bus stop.

"I've got the shelter, so can you carry the bus-stop sign?" Muck called over to Lofty.

"Oh . . . um . . . yeah, I think so," said Lofty, and he followed Muck back to the bus stop.

At the yard, Bob, Dizzy, Scoop, Bird, and Roley gathered around Timmy's box.

"Aww . . . can we keep him, Bob?" asked Dizzy.

"Tortoises are an endangered species. Timmy must be very precious to someone. We'll have to find his owner," said Bob.

"Timmy's owner will be looking everywhere for him," said Scoop.

"You're right, Scoop," said Bob. "I want you and Dizzy to go and find out if any of the neighbors have lost a tortoise."

"Can we find them?" shouted Bob.

"Yes, we can!" Scoop and Dizzy replied as they rushed out of the yard and began knocking on all the doors on their street.

Meanwhile, Roley watched over Timmy as he nibbled on a lettuce leaf.

Dizzy trundled off to Mrs. Potts's house. When Dizzy arrived, Mrs. Potts was in her garden searching under the bushes.

"Tommy, Tommy!" Mrs. Potts called.

"Have you lost something?" asked Dizzy.

"Yes, my tortoise," Mrs. Potts replied.

"Oh, we've found him!" cried Dizzy.

"Thank goodness. Is he all right?" Mrs. Potts asked.

"Yes! Come to the yard and see," said Dizzy, jumping up and down.

At the bus stop, Wendy was digging a hole for the signpost when Lofty and Muck arrived with the rest of the parts for the bus shelter.

"Well done! Now, easy does it, Lofty," Wendy instructed as he lifted a piece of the shelter from Muck's back dumper and placed it by the signpost.

"Now for the roof," said Wendy. Lofty lifted the roof panel very slowly.

"Forward a bit," Wendy called to Lofty.

Lofty swung the panel over Muck's head.

"Careful!" shouted Muck.

"**Can we build it?**" asked Wendy.

"**Yes, we can!**" Lofty and Muck shouted back.

"Good work, team," said Wendy when Lofty had put the final piece in place.

Back at the yard, Roley was guarding Timmy's box. But soon he got tired, and he fell asleep.

Bird and Pilchard snuck up to Timmy's box. Pilchard tipped the box over to get a closer look. Timmy poked his head and legs out of his shell. Pilchard was so surprised that she ran to the other side of the yard.

Bird watched the tortoise start to move away slowly. "**Toot, toot,**" he said as he jumped up onto Timmy's shell, trying to stop him from escaping.

But Timmy continued out of the yard! Roley was still fast asleep.

Bob met Farmer Pickles and Travis outside the yard.

"Hello, Farmer Pickles. That's a lot of lettuce you've got there," he said.

"We're on our way to sell them at the market," said Farmer Pickles.

Bird jumped on top of the trailer. Some of the lettuce wobbled and fell onto the pavement.

"Whoops! Be careful, Bird!" said Bob.

"Don't worry, Travis, I'll pick them up for you," Bob said as he scooped up the lettuce.

He didn't realize that he'd picked up Timmy as well! When Bob put the lettuce on Travis's trailer, he put Timmy in the pile too.

"Do you think I could keep a head of lettuce for the tortoise we've found?" Bob asked.

"Yes, of course," said Farmer Pickles as he climbed up onto Travis.

Roley was looking at Timmy's empty box when Dizzy and Mrs. Potts arrived at the yard.

"Where's my tortoise?" Mrs. Potts asked.

"I don't know. I think Timmy's lost!" said Roley sadly. "I fell asleep, and when I woke up, he was gone."

"He's called Tommy, Roley," Mrs. Potts corrected.

Everyone searched all over the yard—except Roley who kept very still just in case he rolled over the tortoise.

"**Tommmmyyy!**" called Dizzy.

Wendy, Muck, and Lofty arrived back at the yard and joined in the search. Farmer Pickles followed them in.

"I might have found just what you're looking for," Farmer Pickles said. "He was fast asleep at the bottom of the trailer."

"Oh, thank you, Farmer Pickles," said Mrs. Potts.

Bob and Roley helped take the tortoise back to Mrs. Potts's house.

"This new run should keep Timmy . . . uh, *Tommy*, safely off the roads," said Bob.

"I thought he looked like a Timmy, but now I think he's more of a Tommy!" said Roley, laughing.

"I'm just glad to have him back," said Mrs. Potts.

"It's been a busy day," said Scoop.

"Yeah, we built a great bus stop, didn't we, Lofty?" said Muck.

"Um, yeah . . . I think so," Lofty replied.

"I found a tortoise," added Roley.

"And I found its owner," chirped Dizzy.

"Aww, I'm going to miss that little fella," said Roley. "But I'm glad he's back with Mrs. Potts where he belongs."

THE END!

Naughty Spud

Spud was gazing up at an apple tree. The apples looked juicy and ready to eat. But he couldn't quite reach them! He jumped as high as he could, but it wasn't high enough.

"Hmm . . . ," he muttered as he tried to work out a way to get the apples off the tree.

Just then Travis trundled past. "Guess what?" he said excitedly. "Bob is going to finish building my shed today. I can't wait. It'll be so cozy."

Bob was at Farmer Pickles's farm, nailing the roof of Travis's shed in place.

"Nearly done," Bob called down to Dizzy. "We can go home soon."

But Dizzy didn't hear. She was busy listening to the music on her headphones!

Spud walked by and spotted Bob's ladder. "Perfect!" he whispered to himself. No one was watching, so he decided to borrow it.

Bob had nearly finished the roof when Muck turned up.
Dizzy was still singing to herself and didn't notice
Muck arrive.

"Muck, where's the ladder?" called Bob.

"I don't see it anywhere," Muck replied.

"Oh, no! I'm stuck up here! How am
I going to get down?" moaned Bob.

Spud propped the ladder up against the trunk of the tree and climbed up. Soon he had picked every single apple on the tree! He got to work eating the huge pile of fruit.

"Mmm, delicious!" Spud mumbled through a mouthful of apple.

Bob used his cell phone to call Wendy, and she and Scoop raced to Farmer Pickles's farm. **"Can we rescue him?"** asked Wendy. **"Yes, we can!"** shouted Scoop. Bob was really relieved to see Wendy and Scoop.

"Thank goodness you're here," he said. "I was beginning to think I would have to sleep up here tonight!"

Scoop raised his front scoop up toward Bob.

"Don't worry, Bob," said Wendy. "We'll soon have you down."

"Jump into my front scoop," cried Scoop.

Bob climbed in carefully, and Scoop lowered him to the ground very gently.

"Thank you." Bob beamed. "I wonder who took my ladder?"

Just then Spud appeared, clutching his
stomach. He'd eaten far too many apples!

"Spud, have you seen my ladder?"
asked Bob.

"Well, I . . . uh, needed a ladder to
reach some apples," mumbled Spud.

"Oh, Spud! Bob's been stuck on
that roof all afternoon," said Wendy.

"Ohhh! Now I've got a horrible
stomachache," moaned Spud.

"Well, it serves you right for being
so greedy," Wendy told him. "Go and
get that ladder now, before you get into any
more mischief!"

That night Spud had a very sore tummy. He went to see Travis.

Travis was so happy and warm in his new shed that he felt a bit sorry for Spud.

"Travis, if I bring you the rest of the apples, can I stay in your shed tonight?" begged Spud.

"I suppose so," Travis said. "But I hope you've learned your lesson!"

THE END!

Travis Paints the Town

Wendy was busy giving out the jobs for the day.
"Bob," she called. "You, Muck, and Roley are off
to finish the new section of road. Travis can
follow you with the road-marking machine in his trailer."

"What's a road-marking machine?" asked Muck.

"It's a machine that paints lines down the middle of a new
road," Bob explained.

"It's important to keep the line straight, so that cars can travel
on either side of it and not bump into each other," added
Wendy.

The team took off for the new section of road. When they got there, Roley thundered up and down, flattening every bump in sight.

"When you're done, we can start painting the road," said Bob.

The busy machines didn't notice that Spud was peeping at them from behind a bush.

"This looks like a lot of fun!" Spud said with a chuckle.

Bob pushed the road-marking machine into the middle of the road and loaded it with thick white paint. Just as he was about to start painting lines, his cell phone rang.

"Hello, Mrs. Potts!" he said. "Really? No, don't worry, I'll come over right away!"

"What's up, Bob?" rumbled Roley.

"Mrs. Potts's fence is broken, and she doesn't want her dog to get out," Bob replied. "I'd better go over there. It won't take me long to fix it."

"Okay, we'll wait here," said Roley.

Bob jumped onto Muck and roared off down the road.

Travis, Roley, and Bird stood in the sunshine waiting for Bob. They didn't see Spud pop up from behind a bush and creep toward the road-marking machine.

Very quietly Spud dragged the machine behind Travis. He unhooked the empty trailer and attached the road-marking machine in its place! Then he slipped back to the bushes. "Tee-hee!" he giggled. "Now, for some fun!"

Spud walked out, whistling loudly, as if he had just arrived.

"Hi, Travis!" he called. "I've got a message for you! Farmer Pickles wants you down at the pond. It's really important."

"I better get going," said Travis as he roared off, pulling the road-marking machine behind him!

As Travis hurried on his way, the road-marking machine bounced along after him, painting wiggly lines all over the new road.

"Stop, Travis! Come back!" Roley bellowed when he saw what was happening. "Come on, Bird! We've got to stop him!"

From behind the bush, naughty Spud rocked with laughter as Roley lumbered off after Travis.

"This is the best fun ever!" said Spud.

Travis rushed to the duck pond as fast as his wheels
could turn. He was so determined to get there as quickly
as possible, he didn't spot Farmer Pickles working in a field next
to the country lane. He whizzed right past him.

"Oh, dear!" gasped Farmer Pickles when he
saw the wiggly white lines trailing behind Travis.

When Roley and Bird
came along, Farmer
Pickles called to them,
"Follow that tractor!"

Wendy was in the office when Farmer Pickles phoned.

"Dear me, white paint everywhere!" she cried. "Don't worry, I'll tell Bob right away!"

Bob was busy hammering the last nail into Mrs. Potts's fence.

"There you go," he said. "That should keep your dog nice and safe!"

"Thank you," said Mrs. Potts, smiling with relief.

"No problem," said Bob as his cell phone rang again.

"Hi, Wendy. What? Travis? Paint everywhere? I'm on my way!" he said.

Travis was a lot lighter than Roley and a lot faster, too! The poor steamroller panted and spluttered as he trundled along after Travis with Farmer Pickles and Bird on board.

"**Travis!**" yelled Farmer Pickles at the top of his voice.

But Travis still couldn't hear them over the roar of his engine.

He raced along the road. As he went faster and faster, the white lines he painted got wigglier and wigglier!

While Roley and Farmer Pickles struggled to catch up with Travis, Bob and Muck were chasing after him too.

"Quick as you can," urged Bob. "We've got to stop him before he paints the whole town white!"

"I don't think I can go any faster!" spluttered Muck.

"Please try, Muck!" cried Bob. "Please try!"

Travis zoomed along the road,
heading across a field toward
the duck pond.

Spud peeped out from behind
a bush to admire the mess.
"Hee, hee, hee!" he chuckled.
"Now Travis is painting the
grass white too!"

Then poor, tired Roley wheezed past Spud. His
heavy machinery clattered and rattled as he trundled
after Travis.

Spud chased after them, laughing all the way.

Bob and Muck raced down the hill toward the duck pond at the bottom.

"Watch out, Muck!" Bob yelled as he saw Travis heading straight for them. Muck tried to avoid the tractor. He slammed on his brakes and screeched to a stop to try to miss Travis.

"**Help!**" roared Travis, swerving sideways. The road-marking machine zigzagged behind him, then came unhooked. It rolled down the road, skidded sideways and turned over. . . .

Farmer Pickles and Roley were next to arrive.
There was a huge puddle of thick, white paint.
Everyone stared at the puddle.

"Just look at this mess," Bob groaned.
Poor Travis was very upset. "I didn't
know the road-marking machine was
hooked on to me. I don't even know
how it got there!" he said.

"I tried my best to stop him,
Bob," panted Roley. "But I couldn't
catch him."

"Spud told me you needed me right away," Travis explained to Farmer Pickles.

"I didn't say that!" said Farmer Pickles.

Behind them, a bush started to shake with laughter.

"Spud!" yelled Farmer Pickles.

Spud peeked nervously over the bush.

"What have you been up to?" Farmer Pickles asked.

"Me? Nothing!" Spud replied, trying to look innocent.

"So who hooked the road-marker on to Travis?" Bob demanded.

"Um . . . it was me," Spud confessed, hanging his head.

"You've got some cleaning up to do," Farmer Pickles said to the naughty scarecrow. He got a big bucket, filled it with soapy water and gave Spud a big scrubbing brush. "Off you go," he said. "And keep scrubbing until it's all cleaned up."

Spud scrubbed and . . . scrubbed . . . and scrubbed. On his aching knees he followed the wiggly lines all along the country lanes.

He cleaned up every spot of white paint.

By the time Spud had finished it was nighttime.

"Can Spud scrub it? Yes, he can!"
Spud said to himself as he headed for home.

THE END!

Dizzy's Bird Watch

"Hey, everyone!" Bob called one morning. "Come and have a look at this! It's a bird's nest! And there's an egg!"

"And here comes the mother," said Wendy.

"We'll have to make sure that no one disturbs the nest, so that the egg can hatch into a baby bird," said Bob.

"Dizzy, I won't be needing any cement today, so
why don't you stay here and bird-watch?" said Bob.
"**Yesss!**" cried Dizzy.

"Can we bird-watch too?" pleaded
Muck and Lofty.

"I'm sorry, but we've got a big roofing
job today. Lofty, I'll need you to carry
the tiles," said Bob.

"**Can we fix it?**"
he asked.

"**Yes, we can!**" Muck,
Scoop, and Lofty shouted.

Dizzy watched the egg very carefully.

"Don't worry, Mommy Bird. I'm going to look after you and your egg, because I'm your egg's aunt!" she told the bird.

Wendy came out of her office to see how Dizzy was doing.

"Oh, Dizzy, you're a great bird-watcher!" she said.

Pilchard came over to join Dizzy. They sat very quietly and watched the bird. Nothing seemed to be happening, so they decided to play soccer.

"Dizzy beats the defender," shouted Dizzy. "It's a goal!" she cried as she pushed the ball into the corner.

Wendy rushed over and just managed to stop the ball from knocking over the nest. "Phew! That was close! You nearly broke the egg," she warned.

Dizzy and Pilchard left the
soccer ball and went back to
watch the egg.

"Look! The baby bird is
hatching," cried Dizzy.

"**Squawk**," croaked the
mommy bird proudly.

"Ohhh, he's so sweet,"
whispered Dizzy.

"Wendy, Wendy! Come quickly!"
shouted Dizzy. "The egg has hatched. And look, the baby
bird is so small!"

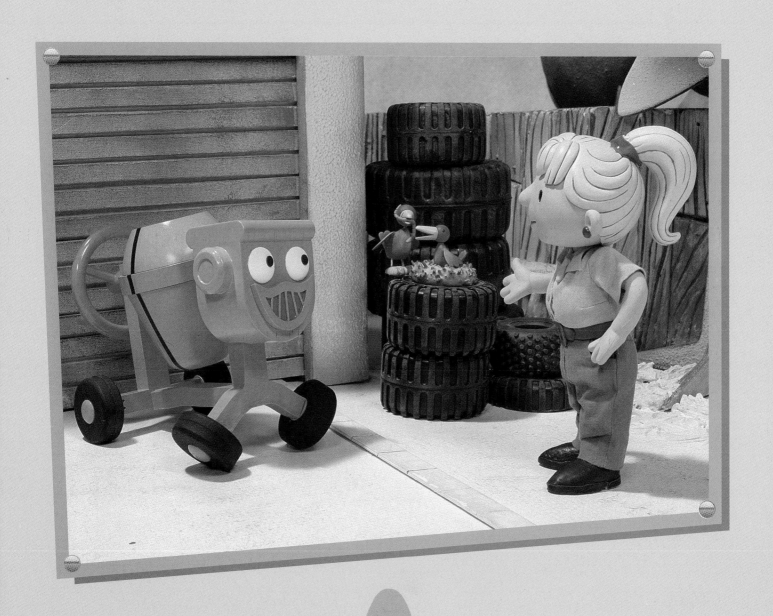

The mommy bird fed the baby bird juicy worms
every day, and each day the baby bird grew
bigger and stronger.

"Ahhh, isn't he growing fast?" said Dizzy.

"Yes," said Wendy. "I don't think it will
be long before he leaves
the nest."

Dizzy was sad. She didn't
want the baby bird to leave.

"You're just in time to see something really special," Wendy said to Scoop and Dizzy one day. "I think the baby bird is going to fly!"

The baby bird tottered on the edge of a pile of tires, then jumped off . . . but he fell to the ground! Scoop picked him up and put him back in the nest. The baby bird tried again. He flapped his wings and this time, he glided up into the sky!

"**Wow!**" cried Scoop and Dizzy together.

When Bob and the other machines came back, they were just in time to see the baby bird practicing.

Suddenly the baby bird swooped onto Dizzy's head and chirped loudly.

"I think he's saying thank you and good-bye," said Wendy.

"That's okay! It was fun bird-sitting you," Dizzy said with a laugh.

"Bye!" shouted the team as the baby bird followed its mommy.

They flew out of the yard and off into the countryside.

THE END!

Wendy's Busy Day

One cold Monday morning, Wendy found
Bob wrapped in a blanket by the fire.
"**A-a-a-a-a-choo!**" he sneezed.
"Goodness, you don't look too good!" cried Wendy.
"I've dot a really bad dold!" Bob said, sniffling.
"You'd better stay at home," said Wendy.
"I can't do that!" spluttered Bob. "We've dot a big
road resurfacing job to do, and it's dot to be finished
by five o'clock."

"Why don't I do it?" said Wendy.

"Dank you . . . **A-a-a-choo!**" said Bob.

"I'll tell the machines," said Wendy as she headed out the door.

Pilchard pushed her food dish forward. "**Meow!**" she mewed.

"I doe you want your breakfast," Bob told her, "but I—" Bob stopped as another huge sneeze tickled his nose.

"**Meow!**" yowled Pilchard hungrily.

"Bob's got a very bad cold," Wendy told the machines. "So he's going to stay indoors until he gets better."

"How will we do the resurfacing without Bob?" asked Lofty.

"You have me!" Wendy said, smiling.

"Hooray!" cheered the machines.

"I'll stay behind to look after Bob," said Scoop.

"Me too," said Lofty shyly.

Wendy hopped up onto Muck's step.

"**Can we fix it?**" she called.

"**Yes, we can!**" yelled the team.

Wendy gulped when she saw the big potholes in the road. "Oh, dear, it's very bumpy," she said.

Roley chuckled. "Hey, Wendy, flattening bumps is my job!" he said.

"Okay!" Wendy said, smiling. "Let's do it!"

Back at home, Bob sat sneezing. "Are you feeling better?" called Scoop from outside the window. "I feel dewwible!" Bob said.

On the town road, Dizzy mixed concrete to fill in the potholes.

Then Muck roared up. "Here it comes!" Muck yelled and lifted the dumper to tip out the sticky road surface.

"I'm right behind you!" rumbled Roley as he moved in to flatten it out.

S-Q-U-E-L-C-H!

Wendy beamed and clapped. "That looks perfect!" she cried.

As Dizzy moved over to give Roley more room she spotted an old soccer ball lying by the side of the road.

"Oooh! Look what I've found!" Dizzy squeaked excitedly. "And Dizzy's got the ball," she cried as she chased after it. "She's racing down the wing. Is she going to score?"

"No! Stop!" yelled Wendy, as Dizzy headed for the sticky, wet road surface. Dizzy didn't hear.

"She scores!" shouted Dizzy as she landed—**splat!**—in the sticky stuff.

"Aww!" wailed Dizzy as she watched her wheels slowly sinking. "I'm stuck!"

"Don't worry!" gasped Wendy. "We'll get you out!"

"How? If we go in there, we'll get stuck as well," rumbled Roley.

"You can't just leave me here to harden like a rock!" shrieked Dizzy.

"Oh, dear," said Wendy. "Let's think about this carefully."

"We can't go **in**," Wendy reasoned, "but Dizzy has to be pulled **out**. . . ."

"I've got an idea!" roared Muck. "Let's get Lofty. He'll pull Dizzy out in a flash! We've got to be quick, though."

Muck whizzed back to the yard with Wendy. "Lofty! Scoop!" Muck yelled, screeching to a halt.

"You two are back early," said Lofty in surprise.

"Lofty! We need your help!" cried Wendy.

"Dizzy's stuck in some sticky stuff, and we need you to pull her out!" said Muck.

"Um . . . okay. Lofty to the rescue!" called Lofty.
As the machines revved out of the yard Bob woke up.
"Scoop!" Bob called. "What was all that
noise? And where's Lofty?"
Scoop wriggled uncomfortably. "Oh,
um . . . he went to see how the
others are doing," he replied.
"Oh, dear." Bob sighed. "I hope
everything is going smoothly."

Things weren't going smoothly at all at the new road. Lofty lowered his big metal hook toward Dizzy's handle. "Get a grip, Dizzy!" he called.

"Got it!" squeaked Dizzy. "**Pull!**" As Lofty pulled Dizzy up he lost his grip, and Dizzy fell to the ground.

"Try again!" yelled Dizzy.

Wendy, Roley, and Muck held their breath.

Slowly Lofty hauled Dizzy off the concrete and gently lowered her down onto the ground.

"Yes!" squealed Dizzy.

"Hooray for Lofty!" cheered Wendy.

"Thank you," Dizzy said, giggling.

Wendy looked at her watch. "Oh, goodness. We've only got half an hour left to finish the road! We'll have to work really hard."

The machines worked as quickly as they could.

With Wendy supervising, Muck tipped the last load of road surface onto the road for Roley to flatten.

DING! DING! DING! DING! DING!

"Five o'clock!" yelled Wendy. "Time to open the road!" Quickly Lofty cleared away the safety barriers. Everyone gathered around the tape that was blocking off the road.

"I pronounce this road open!" said Wendy in a loud voice. And she snipped the tape with a pair of scissors.

"**Hooray!**" cheered the tired machines.

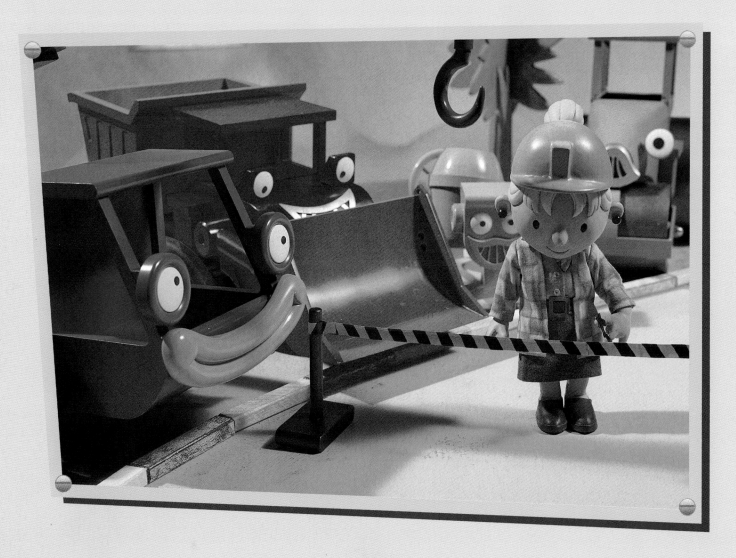

The first vehicle to use the resurfaced road was Travis, with Spud perched on his side.

"We've just fixed the road!" squeaked Dizzy excitedly.

Spud inspected the road. "You missed a spot," he said.

"Where?" asked Dizzy.

"It looks perfect to me," said Wendy.

"Only teasing." Spud laughed. "It looks perfect to me, too! Hah, hah, hah!"

113

Back at the yard, Bob hurried out to meet everybody.

"We did it, Bob!" called Wendy.

"Wad a deam!" croaked Bob. "Dank you all so much."

"Um . . . it's cold out here," said Lofty. "Shouldn't you get back indoors, Bob?"

"Better do as you're told," teased Wendy.

"Okay," Bob said. "I'll have an early night."

Wendy yawned an enormous yawn. "We **all** need an early night."

Later that night, just as the machines were drifting off to sleep, Dizzy nudged Muck.

"Muck," she whispered.

"Huh?" mumbled Muck.

"Wasn't I good at soccer today?" asked Dizzy.

Muck was about to reply, but something started tickling the back of his nose.

"**A-a-a-a-a-a-chhoo!**"
Muck sneezed.

"Now Muck's got
Bob's cold!"
Scoop said.

"Muck, wasn't I good at soccer today?" Dizzy repeated.
"I'm not eben going to answer dat question," Muck said.
"**A-a-a-a-choo!**"

THE END!

Scoop Has Some Fun

"We have lots to do today," said Wendy. "Bob, you'd better get going! You've got those telephone poles to put up. We'll be here, stocktaking."

"What's stocktaking?" asked Roley.

"It's when you count up all of your equipment and make a list of what you have," Wendy explained. "You can start by counting things in the yard, Roley."

"See you all later," said Bob as he hopped onto Scoop's step and left the yard.

"I'll count the pipes!" Roley called. "One . . . two . . . three . . . four . . . um, what comes next?"

"Five!" said Dizzy.

Meanwhile, Wendy was in the office. "Let's see, seven pencils, four rolls of sticky tape, and what's this?" she said as she pulled out a bag from under the desk. "Oh, just Bob's old clothes and a straw hat. I don't think they need to go on the list!"

Scoop finished digging a long row of holes for the telephone poles while Bob called Wendy.

"Hi, Wendy, I just called to say I'll be needing Muck and Lofty pretty soon," he said. "You've found some of my old clothes? I was going to take them to the recycling bin, but I forgot. Bye!" Bob hung up.

"Well done. Time for a break! I'll be back soon," he called to Scoop.

As soon as Bob had gone, Spud popped up from behind a hedge.

"Hee, hee! What are you doing, Scoop?" Spud asked.

"Just taking a break before I start work again," Scoop replied.

"You're always working," said Spud. "Why don't we have some fun?"

Scoop wasn't sure. "What sort of fun?" he asked.

"You know . . . playing jokes!" said Spud.

"Well, it is my break," Scoop said with a chuckle.

And they set off in search of someone to play a joke on.

Scoop hid behind a haystack and left his front scoop poking out. Spud put a bale of hay in the scoop and jumped on top. Soon Travis came up the road.

"Do you like my magic bale of hay?!" shouted Spud. "I can make it fly."

"No, you can't," Travis replied.

"Watch this, then. **Abracadabra!**" said Spud. Then he whispered to Scoop, "Lift me up now!"

Travis couldn't see Scoop at all, just Spud on the bale of hay, floating in the air.

"Ooh! It's magic!" Travis yelled as he ran away.

"Hee, hee, hee!" giggled Spud.

Next Spud and Scoop went to Farmer Pickles's barn.
"Lift me up onto the roof, and then go and hide,"
Spud ordered Scoop. "Hee, hee! Here comes Muck.
Just wait until Muck hears my voice in the sky." He
chuckled. "**Whhhoooaa!**" he called loudly.

"What's that?" asked Muck, skidding to a halt. "Sounds
like a ghost. I'm off!" Muck cried.

"Ha, ha! Now, let's go and find Lofty," Spud called
down to Scoop.

"I've got to get back to work," said Scoop.

"I'll find Lofty myself, then," Spud said.

Lofty was on his way to Farmer Pickles's farm when suddenly Spud jumped out from behind a bush.

"**Boo!**" Spud shouted.

"**Whhaa!**" cried Lofty as he lost control and crashed into a pile of telephone poles.

A pole got caught under Lofty's wheels, and he tipped over. "Help! I'm stuck!" he cried.

"I think I'd better go and get Bob!" Spud said.

"You've got to help. It's Lofty, he's stuck!"
Spud said when he saw Bob and Scoop
farther down the lane.

"This had better not be another one of
your tricks," Scoop warned Spud.

"Honestly! You have to come!"
pleaded Spud.

"Okay, let's go!" said Bob.

"Don't worry. We'll soon have you right-side up!"
called Bob when he saw Lofty.

"All right, all together now!" Bob shouted as
he, Spud, and Scoop all heaved together. Lofty tilted
slowly over and landed back on his wheels.

"Thanks, Bob," Lofty said.

"Thank Spud, he was the one who
came for help," said Bob.

Spud looked worried. "*W-e-e-e-ll*, um,
it was my fault really, Bob. I gave
Lofty a scare, and that's how he got
stuck!"

"Oh, Spud! Well, what do you say?"
asked Bob.

"Sorry, Lofty," muttered Spud.

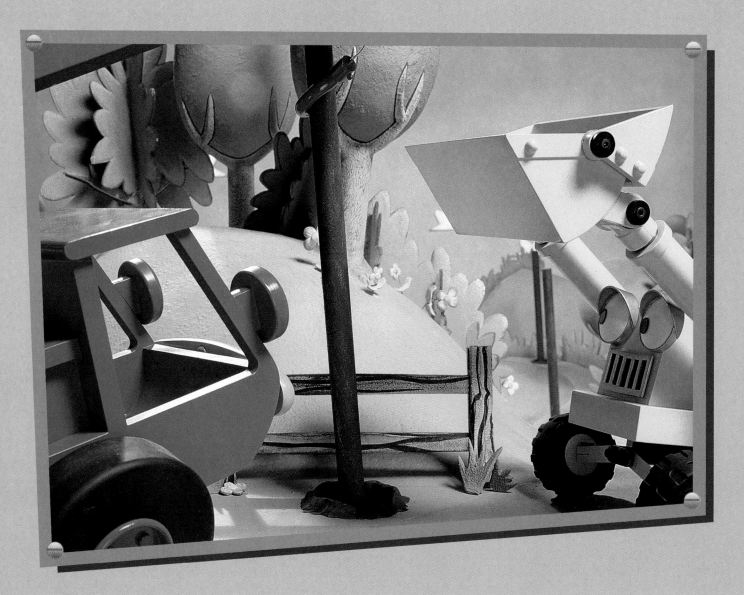

The team got back to putting up the telephone poles.

"That's another job well done, even if Spud's little pranks held us up," said Bob. "Hmm . . . I've got a great idea. I'll call Wendy."

Wendy had just finished stocktaking.

"Oh, hello, Bob," she said. "Yes, your clothes are still here. Do you want them? Okay, I'll bring them to you."

Spud went back to his field to scare some crows. But when he got there, a new scarecrow was in his place! "What's going on?" he cried.

"Didn't Farmer Pickles tell you? You're too naughty. He's asked me to do your job," the new scarecrow said.

"But what about me?" asked Spud.

Then the new scarecrow made a face. "**Blurrggh!**" he shouted.

"**Whhhaa!**" Spud cried, jumping back. The new scarecrow took off his hat and pulled the straw away.

"Surprise, surprise, Spud," the scarecrow said. "This old hat Wendy found sure came in handy."

"Aww, it's you, Bob!" cried Spud. "That's not funny!"

"Come on, Spud! I thought you liked a good joke," said Bob. And everybody laughed.

THE END!

Good-bye!